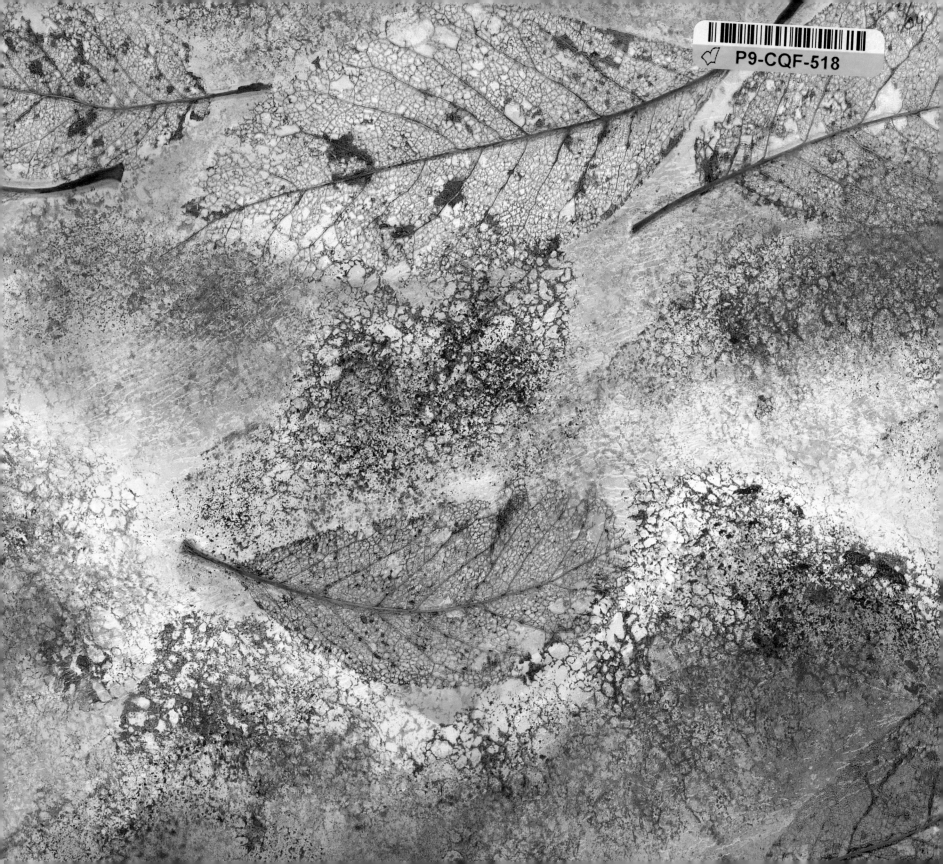

For my mother

First U.S. edition 2004

Library of Congress Cataloging-in-Publication Data

Henderson, Kathy, date.
And the good brown earth / Kathy Henderson. – 1st U.S. ed.
p. cm.
Summary: Joe and Gram grow a garden, with the help of the good brown earth.
ISBN 0-7636-2301-6
[1. Gardening – Fiction. 2. Grandmothers – Fiction.] I. Title.
PZ7.H3805An 2004
[E] – dc21   2003048455

10 9 8 7 6 5 4 3 2 1

Printed in Italy

This book was typeset in Humana Serif.
The illustrations were done in mixed media.

Candlewick Press
2067 Massachusetts Avenue
Cambridge, Massachusetts 02140

visit us at www.candlewick.com

And The Good Brown Earth

Kathy Henderson

CANDLEWICK PRESS
CAMBRIDGE, MASSACHUSETTS

When Gram went to the vegetable patch,
Joe came too.

It was nearly winter.

"Now's digging time," said Gram.
And she picked up her spade
and dug that ground
into big old lumps.

Joe dug too.

He made a hole and a heap

and a squashy place

for squelching in.

And the good brown earth got on with doing

what the good brown earth does best.

Next time Gram went to the vegetable patch,

Joe came too, and there was snow on the ground.

Joe ran and jumped and slid and whooped.

Gram stood and looked.

"Now's thinking time," said Gram,

thinking about all the things in her gardening book.

Joe thought too.

He thought up a snowman.

Next time Gram went to the vegetable patch,
Joe came too, and there was spring in the air.

"Now's planting time," said Gram,
and she raked out the loose earth, smooth as bread crumbs,
and planted seeds in long straight rows.

Joe planted too.
Lots of seeds.
Here, there, and
who-knows-where.

And the good brown earth got on with doing

what the good brown earth does best.

Next time Gram went to the vegetable patch, Joe came too,

and the birds were singing, the trees were flowering,

and the rain and the sun were chasing each other across the sky.

"Now's watching time," said Gram,

keeping an eye on those hungry birds,

and she made a scarecrow and stuck it in the ground.

Joe watched too.

"Gram! Gram!" he shouted.

"There are green spikes coming up!"

Next time Gram and Joe went to the vegetable patch,
it was green all over.

"Now's weeding time," said Gram.

And she picked up her long-handled hoe and grubbed up
all those weeds between her vegetable rows.

Joe pulled up a few weeds too
(at least he hoped they were weeds).

Then he rolled in the long grass and sang.

Next time Gram and Joe went to the vegetable patch,
it was hot, hot, hot.
The plants were drooping and the earth was dry.

"Uh-oh!" said Gram. "Now's watering time!"
And she hooked up the hose to the old tap
and ran it on the plants, sweet as rain.

Joe watered too, mainly himself,
and he gave Gram the second ripe strawberry.

Soon Joe's Ma and Pa took the whole family to the beach,
and Gram and Joe went too.

"Now's resting time," said Gram, stretching out for a snooze.
The sun shone and the breeze blew.

And the good brown earth got on with doing

what the good brown earth does best,
     day after golden day until . . .

The next time Gram went to the vegetable patch,
and Joe came too (of course),
what did they find?

"Oh wow oh wow OH WOW!"

There were Gram's plants standing tall and ripe and lush.

And there were Joe's,

higgledy-piggledy,

tangly,
FANTASTIC!

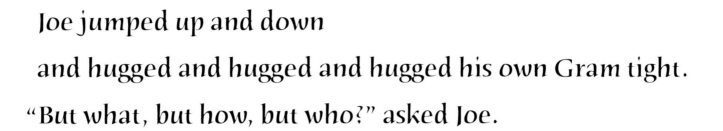

Joe jumped up and down
and hugged and hugged and hugged his own Gram tight.
"But what, but how, but who?" asked Joe.

Gram hugged him back.
"You'd have to ask the good brown earth," she said.

Then she took her long-pronged fork and opened up the ground,
and there were pale brown potatoes like buried treasure,
and carrots and parsnips and beets.

"Now's gathering time," said Gram, filling her basket.
And Joe gathered too – beans and greens,
ladybugs and grasshoppers, dandelions and fat tomatoes,
and he ate so many blackberries
that purple juice ran all down his chin.

And when they'd finished gathering,
Gram and Joe loaded up the wheelbarrow
and set off home, ready for feasting time.

And the good brown earth got on with doing

what the good brown earth does best.